BLUEY

CHRISTMAS EVE
WITH VERANDA SANTA

PENGUIN YOUNG READERS LICENSES

An imprint of Penguin Random House LLC, New York

First published in Australia as *Verandah Santa* by Puffin Books, 2020

First published in the United States of America by Penguin Young Readers Licenses,
an imprint of Penguin Random House LLC, New York, 2021

This book is based on the TV series *Bluey*.

Visit us online at penguinrandomhouse.com.

Manufactured in China

ISBN 9780593384183   10 9 8 7 6 5 4 3 2 1 HH

It's Christmas Eve, and Bluey's whole family has gathered at the Heeler house.

Everyone's already had dinner, which means it's nearly time for Santa to come!

zZZ

Bluey is bursting with excitement! She can't wait to open the presents that are already under the tree.

"**UH-UH-UH**. No peeking at those presents," warns Dad.

"Why not?" asks Bluey.

"Because Santa doesn't give presents to naughty kids," says Dad.

Muffin wants to know how Santa gets in when there's no chimney.

"Maybe he uses the veranda," suggests Bluey.

Bingo bursts out from behind the presents.
"Let's play **veranda santa!**"

YEAH!

Muffin jumps off the chair and lands on her dad's belly.

"Muffin, quick, you have
to say sorry," says Bingo.

"Santa's watching!"
reminds Bluey.

AGHH!
I'M SORRY!

Now it's time to play the game! Bluey suggests Dad can be Veranda Santa, and the kids rush into bed and pretend to be asleep.

"Okay, it's Christmas in the morning. Remember, **NO PEEKING** or **NO PRESENTS!**" calls Dad as he walks out the door.

Dad **TIPTOES** across the veranda and into the room.

Bingo giggles with excitement, and Bluey opens one eye. "Was that a peek?" asks Dad.

Bluey shuts her eye
and shakes her head.
"It wasn't a peek!"

"**HO, HO,** and **HO**," says Dad
as he slips the presents
under the pillows.

It's morning! Veranda Santa has left something under everyone's pillow.

"HOORAY!" cry the kids.

I GOT A SNOW GLOBE!

I GOT SHAVING CREAM!

I GOT A PENCIL CASE!

"Hey, that's my pencil case," yells Bingo, snatching it from Bluey.

"Yeah, but it's Bluey's for the game," says Dad. "She'll give it back after."

Bingo apologizes, but Bluey doesn't want to accept her sorry.

"Why should I?" asks Bluey.

"Because Santa won't bring you any presents!" explains Bingo.

SANTA LIKES CHILDREN WHO ACCEPT SORRYS.

"Okay, fine!" says Bluey and takes the pencil case.

Now it's Bluey's turn to be Veranda Santa.
She grabs the hat and walks to the door.

NIGHT, NIGHT, KIDS. NO PEEKING OR NO PRESENTS.

"We won't!" they
chorus from the bed.

Bluey **TIPTOES** across the veranda and into the room.
She reaches the bed and . . .

HO! HO! HO!

16

"Naughty children! You **peeked** at Santa," she scolds.
"No presents for you. I'm going to throw these in the bin!"

Bluey walks away, but the trio jump out of bed to protest.

Muffin, Bingo, and Dad all put on their very best please faces.

"We're sorry, Santa," says Bingo.

"**PLEASE** will you accept our sorry?" asks Dad.

"Hmmm." Bluey thinks for a moment, then decides she will.

"I sure am a very nice child!" says Bluey. "If I were the real Santa, I'd give me **LOTS** of presents!"

19

It's Bingo's turn now, and Socks rushes in to be her helper.
As Bingo goes to hand out the presents, Dad scoops her up . . .

OH MY TEDDY BEAR.

RRRRUFF!

Bluey copies Dad and
picks up Socks. But
Socks is frightened
and nips Bluey.

"Socks bit me!" yells Bluey.

Dad explains to Socks that it's not nice to bite people. But that's not enough for Bluey.

"She's not even saying sorry!" cries Bluey.

Dad shakes his head. "Socks is only one and doesn't know any better. Let's keep playing."

FINE!

21

Bluey **TIPTOES** across the veranda and into the room.

She creeps across the bed, avoiding grabby hands to deliver the presents. "**HO, HO, HO** and . . ."

Bluey yells, **"CHRISTMAS!"**

Everyone looks under their pillow for a present.

I GOT UNDERPANTS!

I GOT ONE OF THESE!

I GOT BAKED BEANS!

But there is nothing under Socks's pillow.

"Bluey!" scolds Dad as Socks runs from the room.

"But she bit me and didn't say **SORRY!**" huffs Bluey.

Afterward, Mum and Dad find Bluey in the living room. "Bluey, I think you should say sorry to Socks," says Dad.

"I was teaching her that Santa doesn't give you presents if you're not nice," declares Bluey.

"That's not the reason to be nice to people," explains Mum.

"Then what **IS** the reason?" asks Bluey.

Mum and Dad show Bluey that Socks is sitting outside on her own, crying.

"Imagine if Socks did to you what you did to her," says Dad.

Bluey looks at Socks and thinks . . .

. . . She realizes she would be sad, too.

"Hi, Socks. I'm sorry I didn't give you any presents. I was mad because you didn't say sorry," says Bluey.

Socks gives Bluey a lick, accepting the sorry in her own way.

There's time for one last game of Veranda Santa.

"Okay, night, kids. Remember, **NO PEEKING** or **NO PRESENTS**," says Dad as he goes to the door.

Dad **TIPTOES** across the veranda and into the room.

HO, HO . . . OH NO!

31